I0640609

Robert Adams

Illustrated story of the Union in rhyme

Robert Adams

Illustrated story of the Union in rhyme

ISBN/EAN: 9783337259464

Printed in Europe, USA, Canada, Australia, Japan

Cover: Foto ©Andreas Hilbeck / pixelio.de

More available books at **www.hansebooks.com**

ILLUSTRATED
STORY OF THE UNION
IN RHYME

BY

ROBERT C. ADAMS

AUTHOR OF " THE HISTORY OF AMERICA " " THE
HISTORY OF ENGLAND," ETC.

REVISED BY

HERBERT HEYWOOD

AUTHOR OF " THE TWENTIETH CENTURY "

ILLUSTRATED BY THE BEST AMERICAN ARTISTS

ALL RIGHTS RESERVED

*This book is published as a subscription book and to be sold only as such.
Any person interfering with these rights will be held
liable therefor.*

BOSTON
A. M. THAYER & CO.
1891

COLUMBUS BEFORE FERDINAND AND ISABELLA.

Christopher Columbus, discoverer of America, born in Genoa 1435, died in Seville 1506.
Discovered San Salvador October 12. 1492.

ILLUSTRATIONS.

ILLUSTRATIONS.

BALBOA AND THE PACIFIC.

PREFACE.

This History of the United States
'Tis not pretended higher rates
    Than Bancroft, Barnes or Lossing!
But to the student pressed for time,
This condensation clothed in rhyme
    'Tis hoped will prove a blessing.

ILLUSTRATED STORY OF THE

UNION IN RHYME.

DISCOVERIES.

About the year ten hundred two, A. D.
1002.
  So Iceland's legends say,
Norwegians saw America
  From Greenland to Cape May.
Four hundred years of silence came,
  The Northmen's trips had ceased,
When Europe's enterprise sought out
  The commerce of the East,
In Christopher Columbus' day,
  A Genoese by birth,
Who, studying navigation, guessed
  The roundness of the earth,   19

And said that Asia might be reached
　By sailing to the West:
Spain's Ferdinand and Isabel
　Gave means to make the test.
They fitted out two caravels,
　Columbus bought a third,
Aug. 3, 1492.　And sailed from Palos, in old Spain,
　With sixscore men on board.
When seventy days of fruitless search
　Had wearied out his crew,
Oct. 12, 1492.　Columbus saw San Salvador
　In fourteen ninety-two.
When Cuba, San Domingo's shore,
　And smaller isles were seen,
He carried back to Spain next year
　The tidings to the Queen.
John Cabot gained from Henry Seventh
　A patent to explore,
And with his son Sebastian found
July 3, 1497.　The coast of Labrador.

FIRST NEW ENGLAND WASH DAY.

Sebastian fourteen ninety-eight
    A second voyage made,
And searched to Carolina's shore,   1498.
    For purposes of trade.
He afterwards found Hudson's Bay,   1517.
    And when King Henry died,
For Spain he voyaged to Brazil,   1526.
    And saw La Plata's tide.
Columbus Orinoco saw,   Aug. 10, 1498.
    In fourteen ninety-eight,
But rivals sent him home in chains,
    To gratify their hate.
The Queen released him, and he sailed
    Once more the westward way,
But ere returning she had died
    And enemies held sway.
Columbus, suffering from neglect,
    At Valladolid died;   May 20, 1506.
His bones beneath Havana's soil,
    In Cuba, now abide.

He made four voyages in all,
  Formed settlements abroad,
But never knew the magnitude
  Of what he had explored.
Discoveries were concealed by Spain,
  And jealous rivals hurled
Such calumnies, Columbus lost
  The naming of a world.
Americus Vespucius,
  A Florentine, made claim
That he discovered the New World,
  And thus it bears his name.
He sailed to South America
1499.   In fourteen ninety-nine,
1504.   And, five years later, made reports
  That favored his design.
Cortereal, for Portugal,
1500.   Six hundred miles or more
Of North America explored,
  And off to slavery bore

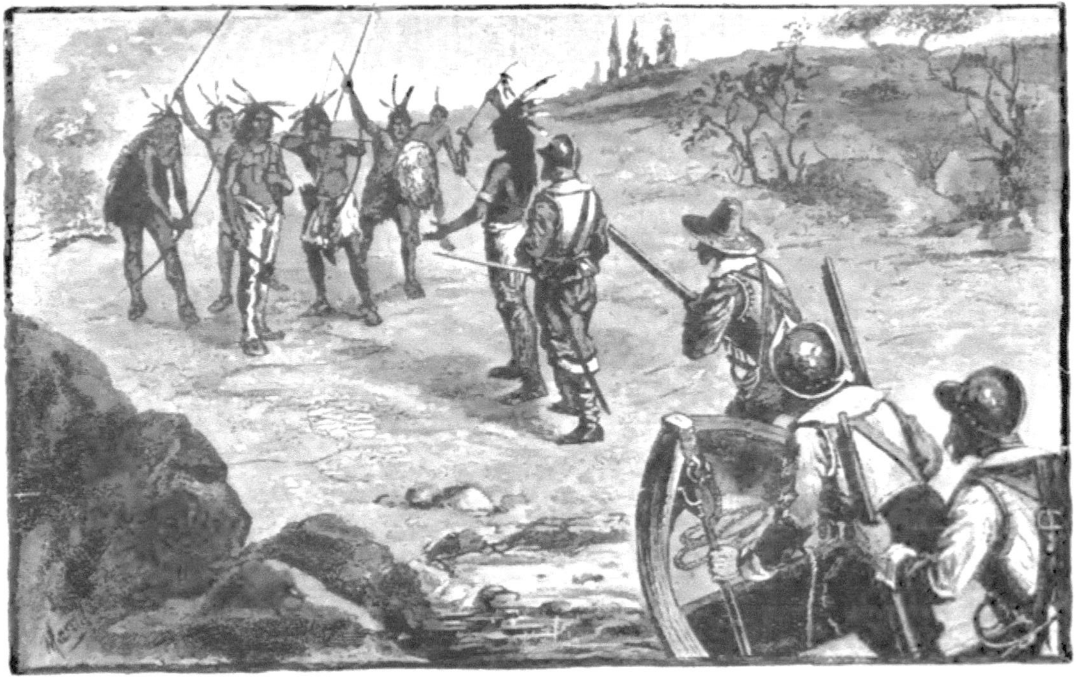

PURITANS AND INDIANS.

Some fifty of the Indians.
  In this unholy strife,
Upon a second rash attempt,   1501.
  He forfeited his life.
The Frenchmen came to Newfoundland   1504.
  To fish, in fifteen four,
They named Cape Breton and explored
  The great St. Lawrence shore.
Some voyagers saw Yucatan,
  And, fifteen hundred ten,
Balboa with a colony
  Encamped at Darien.   1510.
In fifteen thirteen, he the great   Sept. 29, 1513.
  Pacific Ocean spied,
And took possession for old Spain,
  Of all its boundless tide.
Juan Ponce De Leon, fifteen twelve,
  The Fount of Youth to gain,
Discovering Florida, was made   April 6, 1512.
  Its governor by Spain.

1521. But when he came to settle there,
  The Indians defied
The Spaniards, who to Cuba fled,
  Where Ponce de Leon died.

1517. Then Cordova found Mexico:

1518.   Grijalva searched anew,

1519-21. And Cortes conquered Mexico,

1531.   Pizarro took Peru.

1520. De Ayllon, seeking Indian slaves,
  From San Domingo sailed
To Carolina for his prey;

1525.   A second voyage failed.

1523. John Verrazani sailed from France,
  In fifteen twenty-three,
And leaving Carolina reached

1524.   The fiftieth degree.

1528. Narvaez went to Florida
  New settlements to form;
In crazy boats he fled to sea,
  And perished in a storm.

TRAINING-DAY ON BOSTON COMMON.

De Soto, Cuba's governor, 1539-41.
  Came next with crowded ranks;
He marched three thousand miles, and died
  On Mississippi's banks.
One half of his six hundred died,
  The rest resolved to flee,
And, failing to escape by land,
  Built boats and reached the sea.
Jacques Cartier, in thirty-four, 1534.
  Two ships took out from France,
And made attempt in Canada
  French glory to advance.
Next year he made a second trip,
  And on St. Lawrence day, 1535.
Explored the Gulf that took this name
  And up its stream made way.
The vessels anchored at Quebec,
  And, taking boats, he came
To Hochelaga's Isle, and gave
  To Montreal its name.

Again, in fifteen forty-one,
He voyaged to Quebec,
And near the village built a fort,
The Indians to check.

He left ere Roberval appeared,
Who, sent out by the King
To act as viceroy, sailed again
Disheartened, in the spring.

Cabrillo, fifteen forty-two,
Explored by Spain's command,
From Acapulco, steering north,
Along the Western land.

Coligny, Admiral of France,
A place of refuge gave
To persecuted Huguenots
Across the Atlantic wave.

A squadron under Ribault sailed
And reached Port Royal Bay;
A colony of twenty-six
Decided there to stay.

(marginal dates: 1541, 1542, 1542, 1562)

FANEUIL HALL, BOSTON.
"The Cradle of Liberty."

To honor Charles the Ninth, the land
  Was Carolina styled;
But failing to receive supplies,
  They left the Western wild.
Another expedition came,
  Led by Laudonniere,
To the St. John's, in Florida,   1564
  And built a fortress there.
This rousing Spanish jealousy,
  Melendez brought a crew,
Who, settling at St. Augustine,   1565
  Nine hundred Frenchmen slew.
A fiery Gascon named De Gourges,
  In anger crossed the seas,
Secured two hundred prisoners
  And hung them to the trees.
He fled, and Spain retained the land;
  St. Augustine thus rates
The oldest town existing now
  Within the United States.

1576-77.
    For gold, and northwest passages
       To reach East Indian trade,
    Three unsuccessful voyages
       By Frobisher were made.

1578-80.
    In seventy-nine, Sir Francis Drake
       Passed California's coast;
    And John de Fuca, later on,
       Still further search could boast.

    Sir Humphrey Gilbert for his queen
       Made claim to Newfoundland;

1583.
    His little vessel of ten tons
       Went down with all its band.

1584.
    Then Walter Raleigh for himself,
       With patents to explore,
    Sent Amidas and Barlow out
       To Carolina's shore.

    The land was called Virginia
       By England's virgin queen,
    And Raleigh, knighted, sent more ships
       To settle his demesne.

FAMOUS RIDE OF PAUL REVERE.

Sir Richard Grenville led the fleet   1585.
  And founded Roanoke;
But Indian hostility
  They managed to provoke,
And after suffering much distress,
  Were eager to forsake
The colony, and go on board
  The ships of Francis Drake.   1586.
They scarce had sailed when ships arrived
  With bountiful supplies;
And Grenville landed fifteen men
  To hold the enterprise.
Then Raleigh sent more emigrants
  With Governor White, who found   1587.
The bones of all the fifteen men
  Exposed upon the ground.
Returning home to get supplies,
  He left a hundred there,
Among whom was the first born child
  They called Virginia Dare.

1590. Three years elapsed before John White
    The settlement regained;
The colony had disappeared,
    No vestige then remained.
Sir Walter sent five different times,
    But never found a trace;
'Tis thought they joined the Indians,
    And mingled with their race.

1602. Gosnold, in sixteen hundred two,
    Explored and named Cape Cod;
1603. Then Martin Pring, and Weymouth next,
1605.   Maine's territory trod.

VIRGINIA.

The chartered London Company,
    A settlement to form,
Sent Newport out to Roanoke,
    But, driven by a storm,
He found the Bay of Chesapeake,
    Up the James River came,

BOSTON BOYS AND GENERAL GAGE.

May twenty-third, in sixteen seven;   May 23, 1607.
  Thus Jamestown took its name.
Gosnold, projector of the plan,
  And half the settlers died;
The rulers proving weak and bad,
  John Smith was wisely tried.
He organized the colony,
  But, travelling through the lands,
Was captured, and two men were slain
  By savage Indian bands.
Condemned to die, his life was saved
  By Pocahontas' love,
Who, clinging to his neck, detained
  The clubs that swung above.
The settlement was reinforced
  With idle gentlemen;
An accident made Smith go home;
  Disaster followed then;
And as the starving colonists
  Were sailing far away,

Lord Delaware with full supplies
1610.   Arrived within the bay.

1611.   Then Gates came out with working men,
Prosperity returned;

1613   Fair Pocahontas married Rolfe;
Powhatan's love was earned.

By emigration every year,
The State was firmly planted;

1621.   King James, in sixteen twenty-one,
A constitution granted.

NEW ENGLAND — MASSACHUSETTS.

The Plymouth Company resolved
New lands abroad to gain;
An unsuccessful settlement

1607.   George Popham made in Maine.

1614.   In sixteen fourteen, brave John Smith
The region well explored,
And, naming it New England, sailed
To spread its fame abroad.

GEORGE WASHINGTON.

Born 1732, died 1799. Commander-in-chief of the Colonial Forces, War of Independence. Elected first President of the United States 1789.

He came to form a colony
  With sixteen men next year,
But, captured by French pirates, lost   1615.
  His ship and all its gear.
The persecuted Puritans
  Away from England fled ;
John Robinson, in sixteen eight,   1608.
  His faithful followers led
To Leyden, where they formed a church
  And heard Dutch sailors tell
Of favored lands across the sea,
  Where they in peace might dwell.
An embassy, to England sent,
  Got leave to colonize,
And London merchants furnished means
  To purchase their supplies.
Although the *Speedwell's* courage failed,
  The *Mayflower* spread her sails
At Plymouth, with a hundred souls,   Sept. 6, 1620.
  And braved the Atlantic gales.

They sailed nine weeks and safely reached
   The harbor of Cape Cod,
Rejoicing in a land that gave
   Freedom to worship God.
They gathered in the cabin there,
   A constitution wrote,
And made John Carver governor,
   By universal vote.
They set their feet on Plymouth Rock,
   December twenty-second,
In sixteen twenty; from this date
   The settlement is reckoned.
The governor and nearly half
   Of all the little nation,
Ere summer came had lost their lives
   Through sickness and privation.
Their hopes were dull, when Samoset,
   An Indian chief, appeared,
And shouting, "Welcome, Englishmen!"
   Their drooping spirits cheered.

1620.

1621.

THE MINUTE MEN.

A treaty, formed with Massassoit,
  For fifty years was kept;
And Bradford thirty years was made
  The ruler's place to accept.

A colony, at Weymouth formed,
  Aroused the Indian foe;
Miles Standish to the rescue came   1623.
  In time to avert the blow.

John Endicott, with five score men,   1628.
  To Salem came to stay,
And there he formed the colony
  Of Massachusetts Bay.

Next year "three godly ministers"   1629.
  Two hundred settlers brought
From England, and on Charlestown Neck
  A residence they sought.

John Winthrop fifteen hundred brought,
  In sixteen hundred thirty,
And Boston, with its neighboring towns,   1630.
  Was settled by this party.

1635. Three thousand settlers came one year,
    Among them Henry Vane,
1636. Who served a year as governor
    And sailed for home again.
The Puritans most highly prized
    The freedom they had bought,
But yet denied to other men
    The liberty of thought.
In Salem, Roger Williams preached
    That rulers had no right
To dictate in religious things,
    Man's conscience is his light.
1635. He, banished, fled to wintry wilds
    Where savages abounded;
Canonicus then gave him land;
1637. Rhode Island thus was founded.
Anne Hutchinson's peculiar creed
    Caused Boston much dissension;
1637. Imprisonment, then banishment,
    Were meted by convention.

WASHINGTON AT VALLEY FORGE.

New England's colonies were joined, 1643.
  In sixteen forty-three,
Except Rhode Island, which had failed
  With Plymouth to agree.
Ten Quakers, who had crossed the sea,
  Were back to England shipped, 1656.
But others came, and, for their faith,
  Were hanged, imprisoned, whipped.
But when the persecutions ceased, 1661.
  The Quaker zeal was staid,
And seconding John Eliot's work,
  They gave the Indians aid.
Good Massassoit kept the peace;
  By English growth made sore,
His son the friendly treaties broke,
  And waged King Philip's war. 1675.
New England's fiercest Indian tribes
  This wrathful chieftain led,
And fearful slaughter raged a year,
  Till Church cut off his head. 1676.

Two judges, who condemned Charles First,
Were sheltered in the land;
1660. This brought a Navigation Act
From Charles the Second's hand.

It favored England in their trade,
And hindered foreign barter,
1683. And Charles, to gain control, annulled
The Massachusetts charter.

1686. James Second all New England's States
A royal province made;
1686. Sir Edmund Andros was sent out
The government to aid.

But when King James had lost his throne,
This tyrant went to jail,
1689 And Boston's patriots sent him home,
With fifty more, by sail.

In three years more Sir William Phipps
1692. Was sent his place to fill;
New England's colonies remained
A royal province still.

INDEPENDENCE HALL, PHILADELPHIA.
Place where the Declaration of Independence was signed July 4, 1776.

Belief in witchcraft cursed the land   1692.
  In sixteen ninety-two;
Wise Cotton Mather and great men
  Declared the doctrine true.
In Salem persecution raged,
  In jail were hundreds flung,
By torture fifty-five confessed,
  And twenty folks were hung.

NEW YORK.

The Dutch sent Henry Hudson out,   1609.
  Who came to New York Bay,
And up the river Hudson made
  For sixty leagues his way.
In sixteen thirteen Adrian Block   1613.
  First Hell Gate's passage made ;
And many ships then came to seek
  The fur and peltry trade.
The Dutch East India Company,   1623.
  In sixteen twenty-three,

Sent thirty families of Walloons
  With May across the sea.

These people were French Protestants
  Who into Holland fled;

1626. Eight families formed Albany,
  The rest at Brooklyn stayed.

In twenty-six came Minuit,
  Dutch power to augment;

The Indians sold Manhattan Isle,
  Ten acres for a cent.

Fierce warfare with the Indians
  Gave twenty years of care;

1655. The Dutch by force of arms subdued
  The Swedes of Delaware.

1664. An English fleet arrived in port,
  In sixteen sixty-four,

Demanding for the Duke of York
  Surrender of the shore.

The Council yielded up the place
  Against Stuyvesant's pleas;

PRINTER

ERRAND BOY

AT THE COURT OF FRANCE

BEN FRANKLIN

EXPERIMENTING

JOURNEY TO PHILADELPHIA

The English flag above New York
  Then floated on the breeze.
The Dutch, in sixteen seventy-three,   1673.
  Through treason gained the town;
But gave it, after sixteen months,
  Again to England's crown.
The tyranny of governors
  Made Leisler take the rule,
Whom Sloughter most unjustly hung,   1691.
  By liquor made a fool.
Against West India pirate craft
  They sent out Captain Kidd,   1699.
Who hoisted up the pirate's flag,
  " And wickedly he did."
In politics the Democrats
  Were led by Rip Van Dam,   1732.
And party strife, for many years,
  Kept passions in a flame.
The people feared the " Negro Plot,"   1741.
  To burn New York for gold,

And nearly eighty colored folks
   Were hanged, or burned, or sold.

MARYLAND.

Lord Maryland secured a grant
   Beyond Potomac's shore;
1634. The persecuted Catholics,
   In sixteen thirty-four,
From England to St. Mary's came
   In search of toleration,
1635-45. And Maryland was opened to
   The oppressed of every nation.
Dissension came, and Clayborne twice
   Against the crown rebelled;
The Protestants unjustly used
   The powers that they held.
In civil wars and party strifes
   The time was largely spent,
1715. Until the fourth Lord Baltimore
   Secured the government.

THOMAS JEFFERSON.

Born 1743, died 1826, framed Declaration of Independence June 28, 1776, signed July 4, 1776, elected third President of the United States 1801.

CONNECTICUT.

The river of Connecticut
  Was found by Adrian Block,   1614.
In sixteen fourteen, and the Dutch
  Its trading chances took.
Earl Warwick got a grant of land,   1630.
  Expressed in current notion,
"From Narragansett River to
  The great Pacific Ocean."
He soon transferred his interest   1631.
  To Say-and-Seal and Brooke,
Who towards the region's settlement
  Some active measures took.
In sixteen hundred thirty-three
  Holmes' colony was made   1633.
At Windsor; Steele then brought a band 1635.
  Who near to Hartford stayed.
A hundred more, from Boston, joined   1636.
  Their friends the following year,

"The light of Western Churches" styled,
   Good Hooker gave them cheer.

1636. John Winthrop built the Saybrook fort,
   And made a colony there,
Determined that these fertile lands
   The Dutchmen should not share.

1637. The Pequod War distressed the land,
   And thirty men were slain;
The Narragansetts were induced
   As allies to remain
By Roger Williams, and they joined
   The troops of Captain Mason,
Inflicting on the Pequod tribe
   Complete extermination.

John Davenport, with London friends,
1638.   Arranged New Haven's site;
Church members were the only men
   Who held the voter's right.

1662. A Royal Charter was obtained
   In sixteen sixty-two;

READING THE DECLARATION OF INDEPENDENCE ON THE FOURTH OF JULY.

The Colonies of Connecticut
  A bond of union drew.
When Andros came with sixty men,
  The charter to revoke,
Brave Captain Wadsworth hid it safe   1687.
  Within the "charter oak."

DELAWARE.

The Dutch came out to Delaware   1631.
  In sixteen thirty-one,
But savages destroyed them all
  Before a year was gone.
Then Swedes established colonies   1638.
  In sixteen thirty-eight;
But Dutch and English finally,
  Secured the little State.

NEW JERSEY.

New Jersey's settlement was made   1664.
  In sixteen sixty-four,

And Carteret and Berkeley both
 The landed titles bore.

1676. West Jersey passed within the hands
 Of Quakers and of Penn,

Until in seventeen hundred two,

1702. It joined the East again,

And both were subject to New York
 Till seventeen thirty-eight,

1738. When Governor Lewis Morris ruled
 New Jersey separate.

THE CAROLINAS.

1663. Lord Clarendon and seven friends,
 In sixteen sixty-three,

Secured the Carolina lands
 From Charles the Second — free.

The colonies of Albemarle
 And Carteret were formed;

To Charleston's genial settlement
 Both Dutch and Huguenots swarmed.

JOHN QUINCY ADAMS.

Born 1767, died 1848, elected senator from Massachusetts 1803, appointed Minister to France, Secretary of State 1817, Monroe Administration; President, 1825.

In seventeen hundred twenty-nine
  A separation came;   1729.
Then Carolina, North and South,
  The royal rule proclaim.

PENNSYLVANIA.

Good William Penn, in eighty-two,   1682.
  Brought out a chartered right,
And bargained fairly with the Swedes
  For Philadelphia's site.
He paid respect to Indian tribes,
  And treated them as men;
The Indians in turn resolved
  "To live in love with Penn."
He went to England to reside   1684.
  In sixteen eighty-four,
But came again in ninety-nine,   ·699·
  Remaining two years more.
His heirs controlled the government
  Till revolution came;

1779.
The State of Pennsylvania
Then paid them for their claim.

GEORGIA.

1733.
Good General Oglethorpe came out,
In seventeen thirty-three,
And at Savannah formed a home,
Where debtors might be free.

KING WILLIAM'S WAR.

King William's costly war with France
For seven years was waged,

1680.
Canadian, French, and Indian bands
The colonists enraged.

1690.
Schenectady, and other towns,
These foes attacked and burned;
The colonists were then aroused,
And warfare was returned.

1690.
Port Royal, in Acadia,
Was plundered by a fleet,

CHARGING AN INDIAN CAMP.

But forces sent to Canada
   Encountered sore defeat.

QUEEN ANNE'S WAR.

Queen Anne's War made with France
     and Spain,   1702.
   In seventeen hundred two,
Awoke the French and Indian
   Hostilities anew.
The town of Deerfield was destroyed,   1704.
   And all the frontier flamed;
Port Royal, by the colonists seized,
   Annapolis was named.   1710.
South Carolina fruitlessly   1702.
   Attacked St. Augustine;
A British fleet and troops were sent
   To Boston by the Queen,
And led by Walker made attempt.   1711.
   Again to take Quebec:

Eight ships were lost; nine hundred **men**
  All perished in the wreck.

KING GEORGE'S WAR.

For thirty years repose was had,
  Till seventeen forty-four,
When France and England broke the peace
1744   And caused King George's War.
The English captured Louisburg,
  But gave it back again,
And failing to make boundaries,
  Let cause of war remain.

FRENCH-INDIAN WAR AND REVOLUTION.

1754   This brought the French and Indian War,
  Disputed lands to gain,
Which sixteen million dollars cost,
  And thirty thousand **men.**
1755   Defeat was met at Fort du Quesne,
  And Braddock lost his life;

THE BATTLE OF BUENA VISTA.
"Down the hills of Angostura still the storm of battle rolls;
Blood is flowing, men are dying; God have mercy on their souls!"

George Washington then showed his skill,
  Retreating from the strife.
In fifty-eight he led the attack   1758.
  Retrieving this disgrace,
And Pittsburg, named for William Pitt,
  Now stands upon the place.
Crown Point, Ticonderoga, both   1759.
  Were yielded by the foe,
Niagara was then obtained   1759.
  By Johnson and Prideaux.
Acadia and Louisburg,   1757.
  With all Cape Breton's isle,
Were gained; and Wolfe secured Quebec,   1759.
  Expiring with a smile.
The Paris treaty closed the war,   1763.
  In seventeen sixty-three,
And England held the continent
  Across from sea to sea.
The thirteen colonies progressed
  In wealth and population,

Oppressions of the parent land
Aroused their indignation.

Their manufactures were suppressed,
All foreign trade prevented,

And taxes laid by parliaments,
Where none were represented.

Their homes were searched by officers
With Writings of Assistance:

James Otis gave the trumpet call
That roused the first resistance.

1765.   ·   The Stamp Act stirred the populace,
And mobs defied the law;

The Sons of Liberty combined,
And home-made clothes they wore.

The English merchants losing trade,
1766.   The Stamp Act was repealed;

Then William Pitt and Edmund Burke
Their love of right revealed.

On colors, paper, glass and tea
1767.   New taxes soon were laid,

DANIEL WEBSTER.
Born 1782, Died 1852. Orator and Statesman.

And Boston had to tolerate
  An English Board of Trade.
Then England sent some soldiers out,
  And passed the Mutiny Act,
Which ordered colonists to provide
  All things the soldiers lacked.
Two regiments, with General Gage,   768.
  On Boston town were quartered;
The State Street massacre took place;   March 5, 1770.
  Three citizens were slaughtered.
The rising of the populace
  Filled England with alarm;
By taking duties off of goods,
  She sought to undo the harm.
But just to keep the principle,
  The tax was kept on tea,
And Boston's patriots emptied out   Dec. 16, 1773.
  A portion in the sea.
Of Massachusetts, General Gage   1774.
  The governor was made.

1774. The Boston Port Bill then was passed,
  Which closed its foreign trade.
A Continental Congress held,
  In seventeen seventy-four,
In Philadelphia, resolved
  The English acts to ignore.
New York, Virginia, and the South
  Were filled with freedom's breath,
And echoed Patrick Henry's cry
  For liberty or death.
Eight hundred men were sent by Gage
  For arms at Concord stored;
The famous ride of Paul Revere
  Soon spread the news abroad.

April 19, 1775. The minute men at Lexington,
  Opposed the advancing host:
The British fired on the band,
  And eight good lives were lost.
At Concord they destroyed the stores
  And hastily returned,

BUNKER HILL MONUMENT, AT CHARLESTOWN, MASS.
Erected to commemorate the Battle of Bunker Hill, June 17, 1775.

For all the country was aroused;
   Each man for vengeance burned.
From houses, fences, trees and rocks
   The musket bullets sped,
And near three hundred men were lost,
   As home the soldiers fled.
Ticonderoga and Crown Point   1775.
   Americans secured,
And large supplies of stores and guns,
   Much needed, were procured.
A second congress met to raise
   An army for the land:
George Washington was authorized
   To take the chief command.
Near twenty thousand fighting men
   Surrounded Boston soon,
And battle raged at Bunker Hill   June 17,1775.
   The seventeenth of June.
The British twice fled down the hill,
   But on the third attack,

The ammunition being spent,
   They drove the "Yankees" back.

Dec. 31, 1775. Montgomery attacked Quebec,
   But fell when first they fired;
They wounded Arnold, Morgan seized,
   The rest in spring retired.

The Heights of Dorchester were armed
   By colonists at night,
March 17, 1776. The English under General Howe
   To Halifax made flight.

Eleven months they'd Boston held,
   While troops besieged it round;
They pillaged houses, rifled shops,
   Profaning "holy ground."

The English fleet to Charleston sailed,
June 28, 1776.   And on Fort Moultrie fired;
The Southern guns replied so well,
   The shattered ships retired.

July the fourth, in seventy-six,
July 4, 1776.   Was passed the Declaration

ABRAHAM LINCOLN.
Born 1809, assassinated April 14, 1865, elected President 1860, re-elected President 1864,
issued Emancipation Proclamation January 1, 1863.

That made the united colonies
  An independent nation.
The English, with the brothers Howe,
  Embarked to seize New York;
They numbered thirty thousand men,
  All eager for the work.
The battle of Long Island brought   Aug 27, 1776.
  The patriots sore defeat;
In fog, they made escape, while Howe
  Was waiting for the fleet.
The British followed to New York,
  And Washington was found
At Harlem Heights. They moved their troops
  His army to surround, ·
But Washington withdrew in part
  His forces to White Plains,
Where soon the British general
  Important victory gains.   Oct. 28, 1776.
The Hessians took Fort Washington,   Nov. 16, 1776.
  And lost a thousand men,

But gained two thousand patriots
  To fill their prison pen.
The troops across New Jersey's land
  With Washington made flight ;
They crossed the ice-filled Delaware
  In boats, on Christmas night ;

Dec. 26, 1776. At Trenton killed some Hessian troops,
  Secured a thousand more,
And safe re-crossed the Delaware ;
  Their loss was only four.
Again he crossed the Delaware,
  At Trenton took his post,

Jan. 3, 1777. On Princeton made a night attack ;
  The foe three hundred lost.
The Howes, with eighteen thousand men,
  Embarked for Chesapeake ;
And Washington departed South,
  The enemy to seek.
He placed eleven thousand men
  In camp on Brandywine,

MRS. MARY A. LIVERMORE.

And stood at Chad's Ford to oppose
  The enemy's design.
The Hessians met them at the front,
  Cornwallis in the rear ;
The patriot troops were put to flight ;   Sept. 11, 1777.
  Their losses were severe.
Pulaski and brave La Fayette
  Displayed their valor well,
But British numbers won the day,
  And Philadelphia fell.   Sept. 25, 1777.
Then Washington, at Germantown,
  Led on a bold attack,   Oct. 4, 1777.
And though almost victorious,
  The patriots fell back.
The British fleet and army gained
  The forts of Delaware ;
To Valley Forge the patriots marched,
  For winter to prepare.
Burgoyne's ten thousand soldiers took   June, 1777.
  The forts on Lake Champlain ;

Aug 16, 1777   But General Stark, at Bennington,
   Resolved to die or gain.

Sept. 19 & Oct. 7.   Two fights at Saratoga brought
   The British woeful fates:

Oct. 17, 1777.   Burgoyne surrendered up his troops
   And sword to General Gates.

   The British, in Connecticut,

1777.   The town of Danbury burned;

Sag Harbor, burned by Colonel Meigs,
   The injury returned.

The Continental soldiers strove
   With hunger, sickness, cold,

And forty paper dollars bought
   One dollar's worth in gold.

By Franklin's efforts was secured
   The sympathy of France,

Who sent a fleet and soldiers out
   The patriot cause to advance.

June 28, 1778.   At Monmouth, General Clinton's troops
   Were putting Lee to flight,

GEN. WILLIAM TECUMSEH SHERMAN.
Born 1820, died February 14, 1891, graduated at West Point 1840, achieved distinction in the Civil War by his " March to the Sea " 1864, and other services.

Then Washington led back the men,
  And Clinton left at night.
The French and English navies met
  Off Narragansett Bay;   Ju.y 29, 1778.
A fight was thwarted by a storm
  That drove the ships away.
The massacre of Wyoming,   July 3, 1778.
  Enacted in July,
By tory troops and savages,
  Description would defy.
The British troops in Georgia took
  Savannah and Augusta,   Dec 29, 1778.
And Prevost's force to Charleston marched, April 27, 1779.
  But, met by Lincoln's muster,
They hastily retraced their steps,   May 12, 1779.
  Retreating to Savannah,
And Lincoln followed in the fall,
  Allied with France's banner.
Attack was made; a thousand men   Oct. 9, 1779.
  And brave Pulaski fell;

The French refused their further aid,
　　Although they'd fought so well.
Connecticut's most noted towns

July, 1779.
　　By Tryon were invaded,
Who, though he burned or plundered each,.
　　His clemency paraded.

Eight hundred men to Stony Point

July 15, 1779
　　Were led by General Wayne,
By strategy and night attack
　　The fortress they regain.

The atrocities of Wyoming
　　Severely were repaid
By Sullivan, who led his troops

Aug., 1779.
　　Upon a vengeful raid.

He burned some forty villages
　　Among the famed Six Nations;
But Indian hatred fiercer grew,
　　By all these tribulations.

American success was great,
　　With ships and privateers;

WE'LL FIGHT
TILL WE RUN
AND RUN
TILL WE DIE!

CARICATURE OF THE MILITIA OF THE CIVIL WAR.

About five hundred British ships
    Were captured in three years.
Paul Jones went cruising with his fleet,
    Along the English coast,
And conquered the *Serapis* there,   Sept. 23, 1779.
    But *Bon Homme Richard* lost.
Then Clinton came to Charleston's siege,
    Which forty days it bore,
Till Lincoln had to yield his troops   May 12, 1780.
    As prisoners of war.
The British made marauding trips,
    Through Carolina's lands,
Which Marion, Sumter, Pickens, Lee,
    Resisted with their bands.
Then Gates marched South, the losing cause
    At Camden to regain;
Cornwallis put his troops to flight,   Aug. 16, 1780.
    And brave De Kalb was slain.
West Point was nearly yielded up
    By Benedict Arnold's treason,

Sept. 23, 1780.   But Major André's captors learned
The secret just in season.
Bad Arnold, by a messenger,
Was warned in time to fly.
Good André rules of war condemned,

Oct. 2, 1780.   They hung him as a spy.
Nat Greene succeeded General Gates,
And Tarleton was defeated

Jan. 17, 1781.   At Cowpens, by the Southern troops,
With Morgan. They retreated,

Jan. & Feb. 1781.   And joined by Greene, the feeble band
Virginia safely gain;
Cornwallis followed, but the streams
Were swollen by the rain.
When rested, Greene resumed the war,

March 15, 1781.   At Guilford Court House fought,
Where, though the British gained the day,
The field was dearly bought.
In South Carolina Greene gave help,

Sept. 8, 1781   At Eutaw Springs gave fight,

GEN. ULYSSES S. GRANT.
Born 1822, died 1885, graduated at West Point 1843. General of Union forces in the Civil War, elected President 1868, re-elected President 1872.

That led the British troops to leave
  For Charleston in the night.
The traitor Arnold led a force
  To gratify his hate,
And burned and plundered brutally   Jan., 1781.
  Within Virginia's State.
Cornwallis taking Arnold's place
  Destroyed ten millions' worth;   May and June, 1781.
Against his forts at Yorktown marched
  The forces from the North,
Who, led by Washington, encamped
  About twelve thousand strong,
Americans and Frenchmen joined,
  A brave and hearty throng.
They fired ships with red-hot shells,
  And forts were battered down;
Cornwallis, seeing no escape,
  Surrendered up the town.   Oct. 19, 1781.
His seven thousand troops marched out,
  Gave up the arms they bore,

And all the patriots gladly hailed
 The closing of the war.
A year the British Charleston held,
 Prepared for warlike work,
Two years their soldiers occupied
1783. Savannah and New York.
Lord North, by English sentiment,
 His ministry resigned;
Sept. 3, 1783. In Paris, seventeen eighty-three,
 The terms of peace were signed.
The struggle left America
 With poverty distressed,
1787. But Shay's rebellion at the North
 By Lincoln was suppressed.
The thirteen States had through the war
 Preserved confederation;
They met at Philadelphia now
 To form themselves a nation.
In seventeen hundred eighty seven
Sept. 17, 1787. They framed the Constitution,

PHILIP SHERIDAN.

Which came in force in eighty-nine   1789.
   By general resolution.
Electors of the United States
   In unity arose;
George Washington for President,   1789.
   With glad acclaim they chose.
By Alexander Hamilton
   Financial laws were made,
With duties on imported goods
   And on the spirit trade.
The latter made the whiskey men
   Against the law rebel,   1794.
And fifteen thousand men came out
   The malcontents to quell.
Two armies in the West both failed
   The Indians to restrain,
Until their country was laid waste   1794.
   Before mad Anthony Wayne.
Affairs of state were well controlled
   In Washington's eight years,

And treaties were with England made,
With Spain and with Algiers.

1797.   John Adams, by the Federalists,
Was President elected;
The alien and sedition laws
His government effected.

America fell out with France,
And many insults bore;
Napoleon gained the Consulship,
1800.   And wisely saved a war.

Dec. 14, 1799.   "The Father of his Country" died
In seventeen ninety-nine;
The homage of the land was paid
Around Mount Vernon's shrine.

1801.   The wise and brilliant Jefferson,
The "Sage of Monticello,"
Was chosen by Republicans,
John Adams' term to follow.

Then fifteen millions, paid to France,
1803.   Louisiana bought;

JOHN ERICSSON.

Born in Sweden 1803, died 1889, came to the United States 1839. He built the Monitor war-ship, which defeated the Merrimac in Hampton Roads, Chesapeake Bay, March 9, 1862.

And Hamilton with Aaron Burr   1804
   His deadly duel fought.

The war with Tripoli occurred   1801–05.
   That pirate dues might cease,

Bombardment of the port secured
   Desired terms of peace.

While French and English were at war.
   Americans carried cargo,

The *Leopard* took the *Chesapeake*,   1807.
   And Congress made Embargo.   Dec. 22, 1807.

Republicans as candidate
   James Madison selected,

And after Jefferson's two terms
   He too was twice elected.

The British roused the Indian tribes,
   Who made attack by night,

At Tippecanoe, on Harrison,   Nov. 7, 1811.
   But suffered in the fight.

The seamen of America
   By England were impressed;

Their ships were seized and all resolved
   These wrongs should be redressed.
A shot against the *President*
May 16, 1811.   Was fired by *Little Bell*,
But civil answer was returned,
   When the frigate's guns were felt.
The War of Eighteen Hundred Twelve
June 19, 1812   With England was declared,
And armaments on land and sea,
   With vigor were prepared.
The British, under General Brock,
   Advanced to take Detroit,
Aug. 16, 1812. And Hull surrendered up the place,
   Disgraced by this exploit.
Another failure was sustained,
Oct. 13, 1812.   Attacking Queenstown Heights;
But these disgraces were retrieved
   By brilliant naval fights.
Aug. 19, 1812. The *Constitution*, Captain Hull,
   Subdued the *Guerriere;*

ADMIRAL DAVID FARRAGUT,

Born 1801, died 1870.   Rendered distinguished naval services during the Civil War, at New
Orleans, Mobile, and other places.

The *Wasp* shot off the *Frolic's* crew,   Oct. 18, 1812.
   Until her decks were bare.

The *Macedonian* struck her flag   Oct. 25, 1812.
   To Commodore Decatur,

And Bainbridge took the *Java* next,   Dec. 29, 1812.
   And burned her three days later.

The daring Yankee privateers
   Excited British fear,

For quite three hundred merchant ships
   Were captured in a year.

The armies sent to Canada
   Returned without success;

But Perry's vessels, on the Lakes,   Sept. 10, 1813.
   Brought Stars and Stripes redress.

The Indians joined the British troops,
   And fought both South and West;

Tecumseh's death, at River Thames,   Oct. 5, 1813.
   Their savage zeal depressed.

The *Hornet* took the *Peacock*, brig,   Feb. 24, 1813.
   And sank her by her cannon;

June 1, 1813.   But Lawrence, in the *Chesapeake*,
　　　　　　　　Fell victim to the *Shannon*.
　　　　　　　　The British ships made ravages
　　　　　　　　Along the Southern coast,
　　　　　　　　And many of the citizens
　　　　　　　　Their homes and fortunes lost.

July 5, 1814.   Scott won the fight at Chippewa,
July 25, 1814. And also Lundy's Lane;
　　　　　　　　McDonough took the British fleet,
Sept. 11, 1814. That fought on Lake Champlain.
Aug. 24, 1814. The British captured Washington,
Sept. 12, 1814. But failed at Baltimore;
　　　　　　　　They captured ships and plundered towns
　　　　　　　　Along the Northern shore.
　　　　　　　　December twenty-fourth, at Ghent,
Dec. 24, 1814. A treaty settled peace;
Jan. 8, 1815.   But Jackson won New Orleans' fight
　　　　　　　　Before the war could cease.
　　　　　　　　To fill the Presidential chair,
1817.   Monroe two terms was sought;

GEN. JOHN A. LOGAN,
Born 1826, died 1886. Statesman and General.

Missouri Compromise was made   March 3, 1800.

  And Florida was bought.   1819.

John Quincy Adams next in turn   1825.

  Four years secured the seat;

Protective tariffs were enforced,

  And brought about defeat.

Then Andrew Jackson served eight years,   1829.

  And put down "Nullification;"   1832.

He let the victors share the spoils

  In office by "rotation."

By limiting the public Bank,   1833.

  All commerce was distressed;

In Black Hawk's War, the Indians   1832.

  Were conquered in the West.

The Seminoles, in Florida,

  By Osceola led,

For years maintained a bloody war;

  They slaughtered Major Dade.   Dec. 28, 1835

Van Buren, by the Democrats,   1837.

  Was chosen for a term;

A crisis came in thirty-seven —

1837.   A great financial storm.

1837-38.   Rebellion in the Canadas
An English war fomented;
The "Northeast Boundary" fanned the flame,
But bloodshed was prevented.

1841.   The Whigs elected Harrison,

April 4, 1841.   Who served a month and died;
And Tyler, the Vice-President,
Was called on to preside.

He vetoed measures of the Whigs;

1842.   Rhode Island quelled sedition;
The Southern Ocean was explored

1842.   By Wilkes' Expedition;

1844.   The "Anti-Renters," in New York,
By force of arms were quelled;

1845.   The Mormons, out of Illinois,
By riots were expelled.

1845.   The Democrats elected Polk,
Though Whigs supported Clay;

HARRIET BEECHER STOWE,
Author of "Uncle Tom's Cabin."

Both Oregon and Texas formed
    The questions of the day.
The Northwest Boundary Line was fixed,
    And Texas was annexed;   1845.
But Mexico still claimed this State,
    And thus to war was vexed.
Then Taylor marched to Rio Grande,
    At Palo Alto fought;   May 8, 1846.
Resaca de la Palma too,   May 9, 1846.
    A brilliant victory brought.
He gained the day at Monterey,   Sept. 24, 1846.
    And Buena Vista won.   Feb. 23, 1847.
Though Santa Anna bravely fought
    Till setting of the sun.
New Mexico was quickly gained
    By General Kearney then,
And California was won
    By John C. Frémont's men.
Then Winfield Scott took Vera Cruz;   March 29, 1847.
    Through several fights he bore

Sept. 14, 1847.   The Stars and Stripes to Mexico,

Feb. 2, 1848.   And treaty closed the war.

1846.   Wilmot's Proviso aimed to keep

          All 'slavery from new States;

          This roused the people North and· South

            To violent debates.

          In forty-eight a workman found

1848.   The California gold;

          And thousands flocked from all the lands

            Where'er the tale was told.

1849.   The Whigs now Zachary Taylor chose,

July 9, 1850.   Who died the following year;

          And Millard Fillmore occupied

            The Presidential chair.

          Domestic slavery now became

            The question of the day,

1850.   And compromises were secured

            By Webster and by Clay.

          The "fillibusters" made attempts

            For Cuba's annexation;

BATTLE OF GETTYSBURG.

But Lopez met defeat and death,
  And roused Spain's indignation.
The Democrats now gained the day,
  Electing Franklin Pierce ;   1853.
The Kansas and Nebraska Bill   May, 1854.
  Made slavery conflicts fierce.
Ten millions, paid to Mexico,
  Arranged the boundary line,
And Perry's visit caused Japan
  Trade privilege to assign.   1854.
Buchanan next was President,   1857.
  And during his four years,
Discussions upon slavery
  Excited general fears.
Some Northern States opposed the law
  That fugitives returned ;
John Brown an insurrection made,   1859.
  And Southern anger burned.
When Abraham Lincoln gained his place,   1861.
  Seven Southern States seceded,   Dec. 20, 1860.

Feb. 4, 1861.   And organized Confederate States,
                By Jefferson Davis headed.

April 12, 1861. Fort Sumter yielded; Northern blood

April 19, 1861.   In Baltimore was shed;
                Virginia was the battle ground
                    To which the troops were led.
                The Northerners sustained defeat

July 21, 1861.   At the Battle of Bull Run;

1861.   At Carthage, Wilson's Creek, Ball's Bluff,
                The South more victories won.
                The North some minor battles gained,
                    Gave Border States their aid,
                And off the seaports of the South
                    Their ships maintained blockade.
                Commissioners, from Southern States,

Nov. 8, 1861.   Were seized on board the *Trent*;
                When England made remonstrances,
                    Apologies were sent.

1862.   Fort Henry and Fort Donaldson,
                With Island Number Ten,

JAMES A. GARFIELD.

Shiloh and Murfreesborough's fights,
  Were won by Northern men.
Antietam's indecisive fight   Sept. 17, 1862.
  Made Lee's command fall back,
And thus protected Washington
  From danger of attack.
The *Monitor* whipped the *Merrimac*,   March 19, 1862
  Preventing great defeat;
New Orleans was forced to yield   April 25, 1862.
  To Farragut with his fleet;
Confederate victories were won
  By Jackson and by Lee;
Then Lincoln's Proclamation came,   Jan. 1, 1863.
  That made the negroes free.
The South at Chickamauga won,   Sept. 20, 1863.
  And Chancellorsville was gained;   May 3, 1863.
In Charleston, spite of all attacks,
  The Southern troops remained.
The Northern forces Vicksburg gained,   July, 1863.
  And Chattanooga's height;   Nov. 25, 1863.

July 1-3, 1863.   The three days' fight at Gettysburg,
               Turned Lee's advance to flight.

May, 1864.   The Wilderness, and other fields,
               Were won by General Lee,

Nov., 1864.   But Sherman made his famous march
               Through Georgia to the sea,

              And Northern armies gained success
               Throughout the South and West,

              While "on to Richmond" General Grant
               With firm persistence pressed.

              Through Carolina Sherman marched,

Feb. 17, 1865.   Columbia was taken ;

Feb. 18, 1865. And Charleston threatened in the rear,
               By Southerners was forsaken.

              On April third, in sixty-five,

April 3, 1865.   Lee out of Richmond fled,

April 9, 1865. And on the ninth surrendered up
               The troops he'd bravely led.

              This civil war, they estimate,
               Three thousand millions cost,

MRS. LUCRETIA GARFIELD.
Wife of President Garfield.

And on both sides, 'tis probable,
  A million lives were lost.
A second term as President
  To Lincoln was secured;
Booth killed him by a pistol shot,   April 14, 1865.
  When peace was just assured.
Then Andrew Johnson measures took
  The Union to restore;
He freely pardoned all the South,
  Except the chief in war.
But Congress, favoring sterner plans,
  His vetoes set aside;
With "carpet-bag" and negro rule
  The Southern States were tried.
Impeachment of the President   1868.
  Failed only by one vote;
The "Freedman's Bureau," "Civil Rights,"
  Were measures of great note.
Atlantic Cable then was laid;   July, 1866.
  Alaska's lands were bought;   1867.

1868.   A treaty was with China made;
               In Canada Fenians fought.

1869.   Now Grant became the President;
               Two terms his valor earned;
               Pacific Railroad crossed the land;
               Prosperity returned.

Oct. 8, 1871. Great fires in Chicago raged,

Nov. 9, 1872. In Boston and the West;
               The threatening "Alabama Claims,"
               Geneva's Board redressed.

1873.   Financial crisis came again,
               Through railroads' bad condition;
               In Philadelphia was held

1876.   Centennial Exhibition.
               The votes securing Tilden's seat,
               Conflicting questions raise;
               Electoral commission finds

1877.   One extra vote for Hayes.
               A railroad strike 'gainst lower pay,

1877.   Produced the Pittsburg riot;

GEN. BENJAMIN F. BUTLER.

Born 1818, Governor of Massachusetts 1882. Rendered eminent service as Congressional Representative from Massachusetts, as member of Impeachment Committee of President Andrew Johnson, and as Major-general in Civil War.

A hundred lives were sacrificed,
  Before restoring quiet.
Five millions and a half were paid
  As fishery award;   1873.
And specie payments through the land
  Were finally restored.
Then Garfield was made President,   1881.
  But fell by Guiteau's hand;   July 2, 1881.
And Arthur filled the vacant place,   Sept 20, 1881.
  As ruler of the land.
In eighty-four the People's vote,   1884.
  Bade Cleveland guide the nation.
He said " whoever serves the State
  Must pass Examination."
And Civil Service long discussed,
  Was put in operation.
Ben. Harrison comes next in power,
  And changes fill the air,   1888.
McKinley makes the tariff higher   1890.
  Chicago wins the fair;

Which is to celebrate Columbus'
Discovery of San Salvador
Four hundred years before.

The working-man and millionaire
Are seeking hard to find
How both can share in harmony
The toil of hand and mind.

The farmers, miners in the West
Ask silver coined for all.

The Eastern men cry " Reciprocity
We want no Chinese wall
'Gainst and Canada and South America,
For trade will make us one —"

And thus, Republics, Empires, Provinces
Unite in one great Union.

Behold amid the breaking dawn
Of twentieth century's morn,
O'er all the western world
One starry flag unfurled.

GROVER CLEVELAND.
Born 1837, elected Governor of New York 1882, elected President 1884.

SUMMARY OF COLONIES AND STATES.

The first enduring settlement,
   Where English people stayed,
At Jamestown, in Virginia,   1607.
   In sixteen seven was made.

In sixteen thirteen, at New York,   1613.
   Wrecked Dutchmen built a shanty;

To Massachusetts Pilgrims came,
   In sixteen hundred twenty.   1620.

New Hampshire's lands were occupied   1623.
   In sixteen twenty-three;

In thirty-four, to Maryland,   1634.
   Came Catholics 'cross the sea.

From thirty-three to thirty-six
   Connecticut was won;   1633-36.

In thirty-six, by Williams' friends,   1636.
   Rhode Island was begun,

The Swedes encamped in Delaware   1638.
   In sixteen thirty-eight;

In sixty-four, Elizabethtown
   Began New Jersey's State.   1664.

1664.   The English navy took New York
                 In sixteen sixty-four ;
             And from this time the colony
                 An English title bore.

             Year sixteen hundred sixty-five,
1665.   Is North Carolina's date ;
             In sixteen seventy began
1670.   South Carolina's State.

1682.   Penn came to Pennsylvania
                 In sixteen eighty-two ;
             In seventeen hundred thirty-three
1733.   To Georgia debtors go.

             These thirteen States the Union formed,
                 And scarce three millions held ;
             Now forty-four compose the land,
                 With sixty millions filled.

             Now four large territories lie
                 Around the Western border,
             And thirty-one new States have been
                 Admitted in this order :

PRESIDENT BENJAMIN HARRISON.
Born 1833, Brigadier-general in Civil War, in 1880 Senator from Indiana, in 1888 elected
President.

Vermont, Kentucky, Tennessee,   { 1791.
                                               { 1792.
    Ohio, Louisiana —   { 1796.
                                               { 1802.
                                               { 1812.
The latter fairly bought from France —
    The next was Indiana.   1816.

Then Mississippi, Illinois,   { 1817.
                                               { 1818.
    With Alabama, Maine ;   { 1819.
                                               { 1820.
Missouri and Arkansas next,   { 1821.
                                             { 1836.
    And then came Michigan.   1837.

Now Florida and Texas next,   1845.
    With Iowa come on ;   1846.
Wisconsin, California,   { 1848.
                                             { 1850.
    Minnesota, Oregon.   { 1858.
                                             { 1859.
Then Kansas, West Virginia ;   { 1861.
                                             { 1863.
    Nevada and Nebraska   1864.
Precede centennial Colorado ;   { 1867.
                                             { 1876.
    Soon North and South Dakota ;   1888.
Montana, Washington crowd in,
    Then Idaho, Wyoming.   { 1890.

THE PRESIDENTS.

1789. 1797. 1801.	First Washington, Adams and Jefferson came;
1809. 1817.	Then Madison; next James Monroe;
1825.	With John Quincy Adam's notable name,
1829. 1837.	Andrew Jackson, Van Buren must go.
1841. 1841. 1745. 1849. 1849. 1853.	Then Harrison, Tyler and Polk took their turn With Taylor and Fillmore and Pierce;
1857. 1861.	Buchanan and Lincoln the honor next earn,
1865.	And Johnson, through murder so fierce.
1869.	Then Grant for two terms was supreme in the land;
1877.	And the seat was next given to Hayes;
1881.	When Garfield had died by a murderous hand,
1881.	Then Arthur to power they raise.
	New York then supplies a man for the nation,
1884.	And Cleveland appears at the head;
1888.	He yields to Harrison's administration, But who shall come in *his* stead?

www.ingramcontent.com/pod-product-compliance
Lightning Source LLC
Chambersburg PA
CBHW021134020726
47500CB00003B/1077